Eric Maddern lives in North Wales, where he has created the elemental Cae Mabon Retreat Centre. As a young man he made a ten-year journey around the world, culminating in work with Aboriginal people in Central Australia. Now, as well as writing children's books, he performs widely as a singer and storyteller. Eric's other books for Frances Lincoln are *Death in a Nut*, *Nail Soup*, *Cow on the Roof*, *Earth Story* and *Life Story*, *The Fire Children*, *The King with Horse's Ears*, *Spirit of the Forest*, *Rainbow Bird* and *The King and the Seed*. His latest CD of songs – '*Rare and Precious Earth*' – came out in 2008.

Adrienne Kennaway was born in New Zealand and grew up in Kenya where she spent many years. She studied at Ealing Art School and the Accademia di Belle Arti in Rome. She loves painting animals, and learned how to scuba dive in order to paint tropical marine fish. Adrienne won the Kate Greenaway Medal for her book *Crafty Chameleon*. Her other books for Frances Lincoln are *Rainbow Bird* by Eric Maddern, and *Arctic Song, Jungle Song, This is the Tree*, *This is the Oasis* and *This is the Reef*, which are all written by Miriam Moss. Adrienne lives in County Kerry, in Ireland.

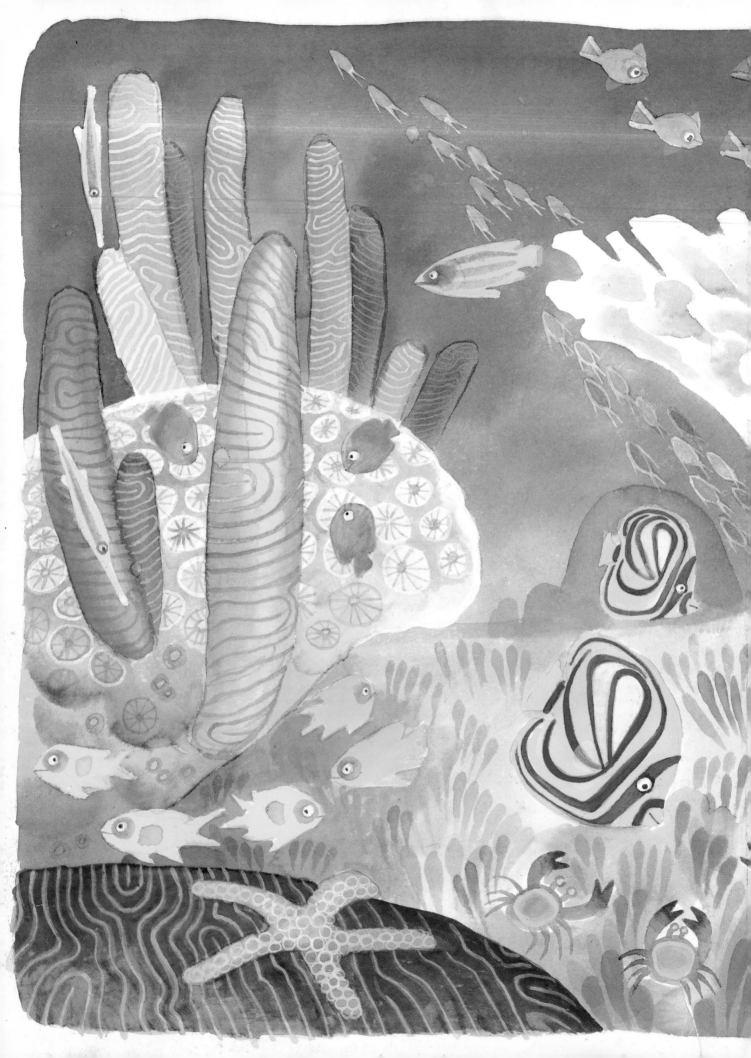

The author and publishers would like to thank Stephen Hall
of Southampton Oceanography Centre for his help.

Curious Clownfish copyright © Frances Lincoln Limited 1990
Text copyright © Eric Maddern 1990
Illustrations copyright © Adrienne Kennaway 1990

First published in Great Britain in 1990
by Frances Lincoln Children's Books, 4 Torriano Mews,
Torriano Avenue, London NW5 2RZ
www.franceslincoln.com

This edition published in Great Britain and in the USA in 2009

British Library Cataloguing in Publication Data available on request

ISBN 978-1-84507-872-0

Printed in China

1 3 5 7 9 8 6 4 2

Adrienne Kennaway · Story By Eric Maddern

Curious Clownfish

F

FRANCES LINCOLN
CHILDREN'S BOOKS

In the warm waters of the coral reef swam many fabulous fish.

But one fish always stayed at home and never even went out to play. This was timid Clownfish, who spent all day in the waving arms of Anemone. Nibbling food, she kept Anemone clean, and the stinging tentacles protected her from danger.

So it went on for a long time, until . . .

one day a different little Clownfish was born.

This baby Clownfish spun into the world and said, "I'm Clownfish! I don't want to spend all my life in Anemone. I'm going to explore the reef!"

With a swish and a swirl, off she swam, looking for an adventure.

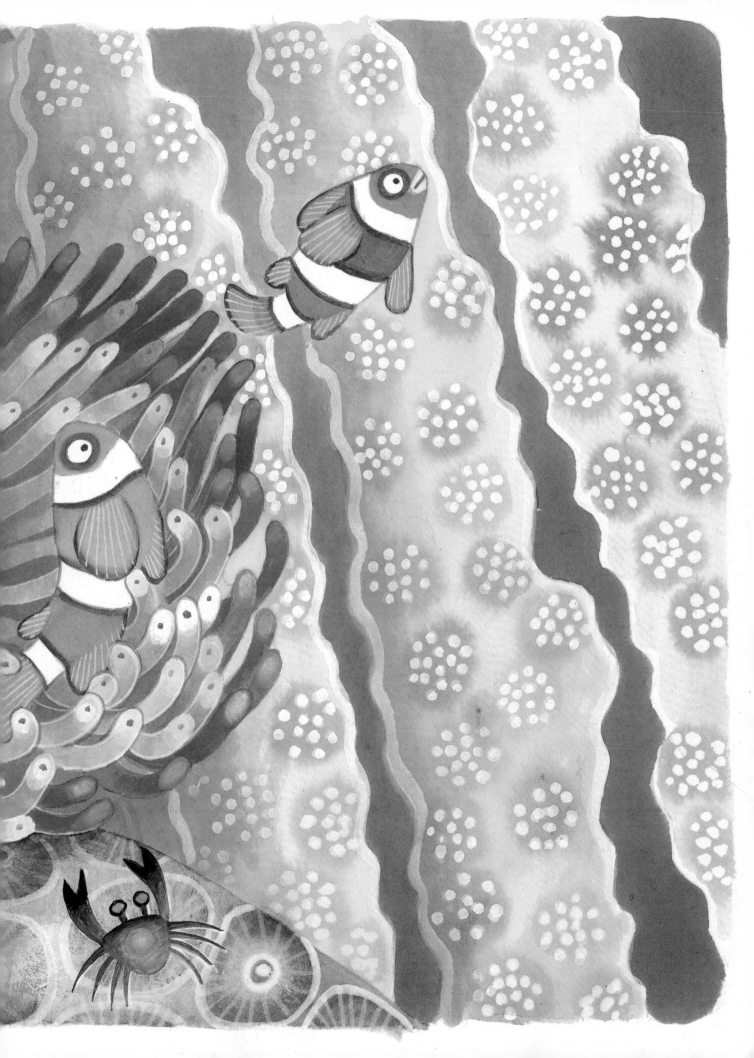

She frisked through the pool, past blue Sea Star, past fans and fingers of coral.
Then suddenly she saw slinky Sea Slug, waving and dancing through the water. "I'd love to dance like that," she thought, and swam up close to join in.
But the water near Sea Slug tasted horrible, so Clownfish quickly swam off again.

Next Clownfish saw a huge spiky fish crunching on the coral.

"Poor thing, he looks sad," she thought. "I'll cheer him up." And she swam close to give him a clean.

But old Porcupine Fish must have frightened himself, because he puffed up like a big prickly ball.

"Whoops!" said Clownfish, and stopped just in time. She didn't want prickly lips.

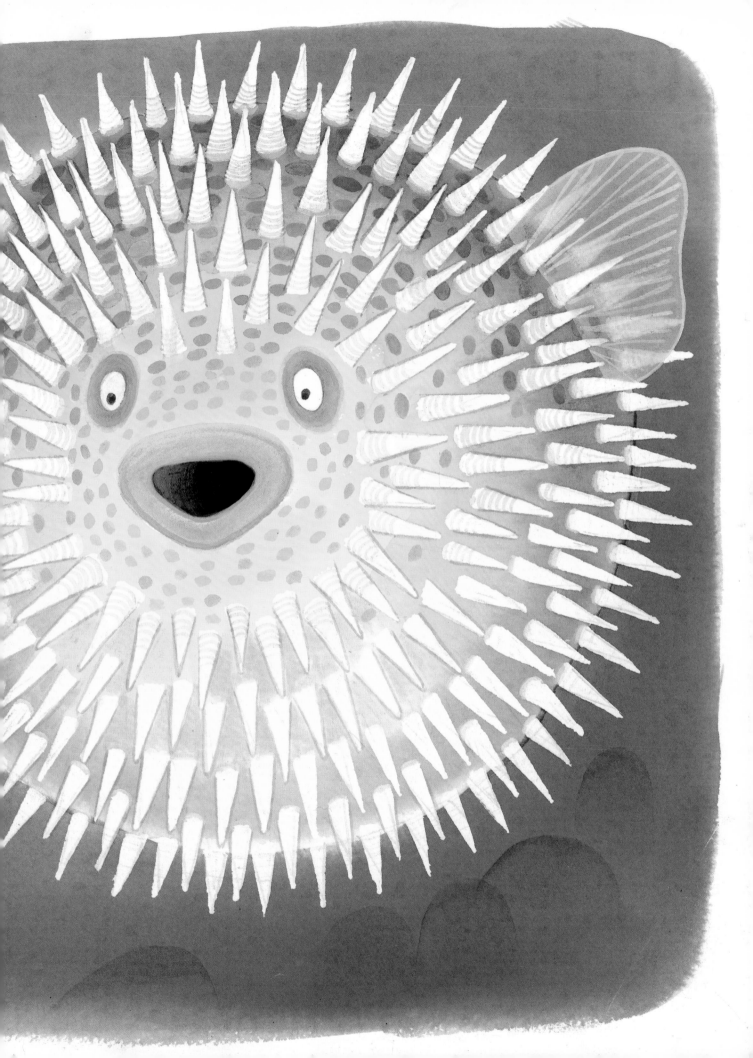

"Isn't anyone friendly?" Clownfish was wondering,
when Spottyfish sailed by with her babies.

"Ah!" thought Clownfish, "can I come too?"
And she tagged along, playing with the little ones.

Just as she was thinking "This is fun!" Spottyfish hurried them into the coral. When Clownfish
looked to see the trouble, she saw . . .

fiery Dragonfish!

Gliding along with her long spines waving, she was quite a pretty sight. But the little fish were all dashing to hide, and soon Clownfish saw why.

One poor fish was stung by a spine and instantly rolled over dead. Dragonfish gobbled him up in one mouthful and floated on by.

Clownfish was frightened by Dragonfish and knew she had to take care. She left Spottyfish and swam around looking for a place to rest.

A big empty shell looked all right, and she was just about to swim in when out shot the claws of crabby old Crab.

Clownfish escaped with a scratch on her tail.

Spiralling slowly through the water
Clownfish came upon Sweetlips.
   She could hardly believe her eyes,
for dancing in and out of his mouth
were two little Blue-Streaked Cleaners,
keeping Sweetlips clean.
   "That's what I do for Anemone!"
she cried. "Please, please can I help?"

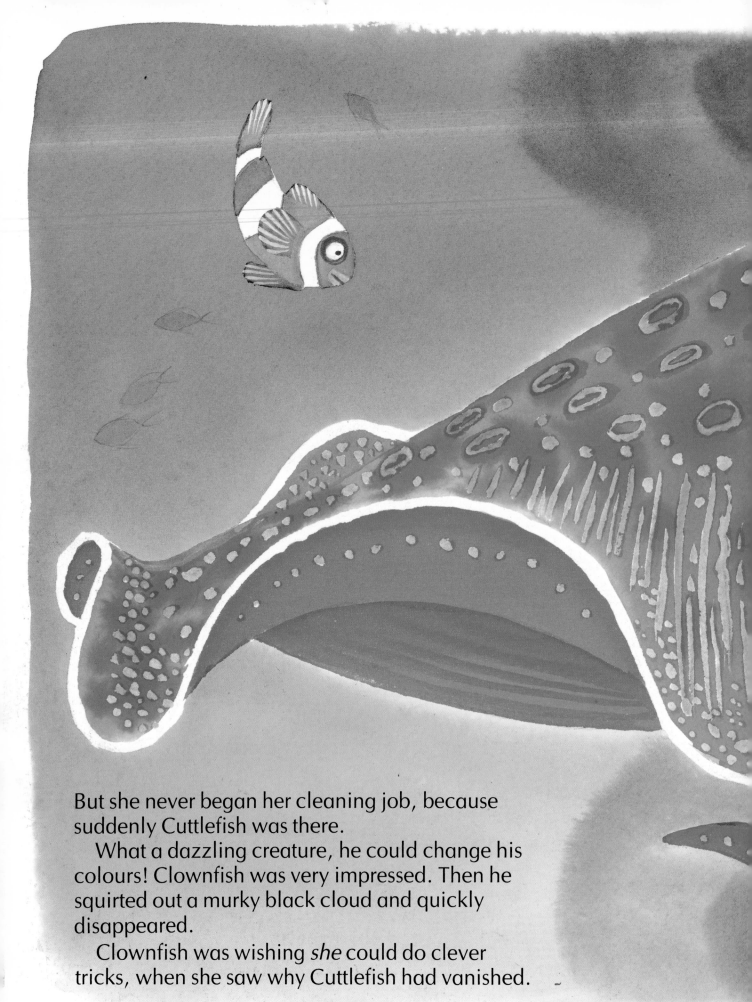

But she never began her cleaning job, because
suddenly Cuttlefish was there.

What a dazzling creature, he could change his
colours! Clownfish was very impressed. Then he
squirted out a murky black cloud and quickly
disappeared.

Clownfish was wishing *she* could do clever
tricks, when she saw why Cuttlefish had vanished.

Through the black cloud the face of Eel came snapping, and Clownfish's heart skipped a beat. Eel was looking right at her. She knew it was time to go.

She turned and swam but was so scared she didn't know how to go straight. Twisting, frisking, looping and drooping, she made the Eel confused. But slowly, slowly his snapping jaws came closer, closer and closer.

Then Clownfish saw the most welcome sight she'd seen for a long, long while.

It was a ring of waving tentacles. Anemone at last. In she slipped just in time and Eel got stung on the nose!

Clownfish was home in her nest of tentacles. What an adventure she'd had!

From that day on, if she saw friendly fish she would lead other Clownfish out to play. But if she saw Dragonfish or the shadow of Eel, she would hurry them all back home.

And so it was that the lives of Clownfish were never quite the same again!

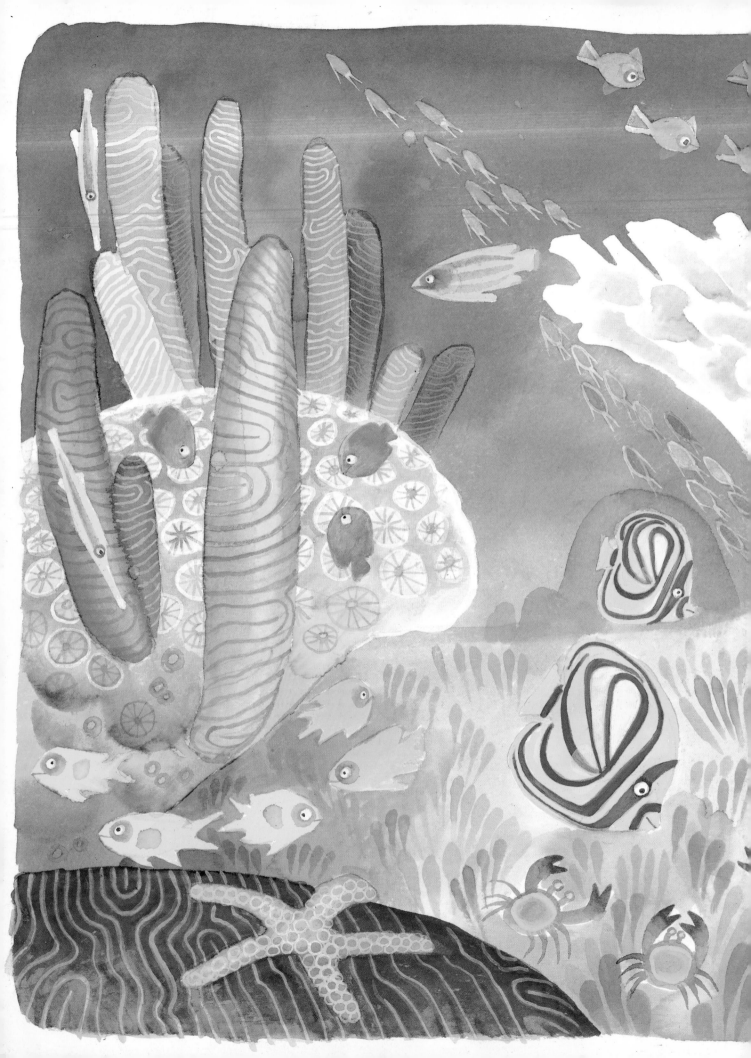

About Coral Reefs

Clownfish lives in a beautiful but fragile environment called a coral reef. Coral reefs exist in warm or cold water, in shallow or deep oceans. The colourful reefs you see in this book are found in warm, shallow waters in the tropical parts of our planet. They are full of life and attract a great variety of creatures. Some spend their entire life on the reef, others call by for short visits during their long sea journeys.

The rock-like coral is formed from thousands of tiny creatures called polyps, rather like the anemone where Clownfish lives but far smaller. Over many years the polyps build a rocky skeleton of calcium carbonate, giving the reef its structure.

The corals can feed by catching microscopic plants and animals called plankton using stinging cells on their tentacles. But they get most of their food from single-cell algae (a primitive plant) that live within them in *symbiosis* – the process where two different life-forms work together to benefit each other (similar to the way that Clownfish protects Anemone from anemone-eating fish, and in return Anemone's stinging tentacles protect Clownfish from Eel.) The algae require sunlight and clear water so these corals can only grow at depths less than 60 metres (about 197 feet).

Shallow water coral reefs are vulnerable to damage from storms and human activities. These include fishing with trawlers, dredging, coral collecting, careless divers, and even deliberate use of explosives and poison to kill or stun reef fish, either for food or for sale to the aquarium trade.

Corals can also be damaged by waste material from building sites clogging the polyps, and by pollution such as sewage or oil that has been spilled. Warming waters can 'bleach' corals, where the coral expels the symbiotic algae, leaving the reef without colour.

Deep water coral reefs lack the symbiotic algae, so can live in cold, dark waters over 3000 metres (about 9862 feet) deep. Many are found in deep waters around the world, but as industry moves into deeper waters even these are endangered, and new rules are being developed to give them protection.

Fortunately many humans care about reefs and are learning more about them so that we can look after them and preserve them far into the future.

There are many websites where you can learn more about coral reefs and the creatures who live in them. Here are a few examples:

http://www.reefrelief.org/kids/
http://www.reef.edu.au
http://www.mcsuk.org/marineworld/habitats/coral+reefs

Stephen Hall CMarSci FLMarEST FSUT, Southampton Oceanography Centre